Tree-
House
Comix
Proudly
Presents

DOG MAN
UNLEASHED

WRITTEN AND ILLUSTRATED BY **DAV PILKEY**

AS GEORGE BEARD AND HAROLD HUTCHINS

WITH INTERIOR COLOR BY JOSE GARIBALDI

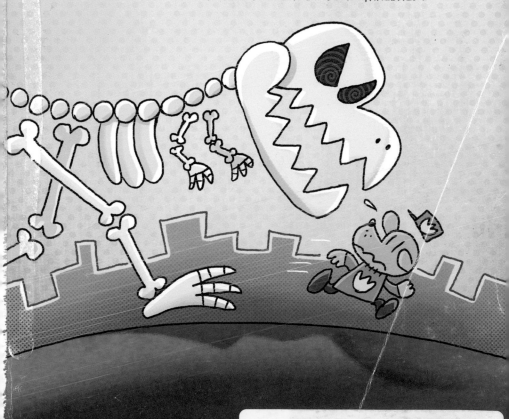

■ SCHOLA

FOR Phil Falco

Scholastic Children's Books
An imprint of Scholastic Ltd
Euston House, 24 Eversholt Street, London, NW1 1DB, UK
Registered office: Westfield Road, Southam, Warwickshire, CV47 0RA
SCHOLASTIC and associated logos are trademarks and/or
registered trademarks of Scholastic Inc.

First published in the US by Scholastic Inc, 2017
This edition published in the UK by Scholastic Ltd, 2018

Text and illustration copyright © Dav Pilkey, 2017

The right of Dav Pilkey to be identified as the author and
illustrator of this work has been asserted by him

ISBN 978 1407 18660 3

A CIP catalogue record for this book
is available from the British Library.

Printed by Bell and Bain Ltd, Glasgow
Papers used by Scholastic Children's Books are made
from wood grown in sustainable forests.

5 7 9 10 8 6

www.scholastic.co.uk

www.pilkey.com

ChapTers

DOG MAN
... our story thus far...

Hi, everybody! Welcome to our second DOG MAN novel!

This comic introduction will help ya get caught up on the epicness!

In a world where evil cats wreak Havoc on the innocent...

Haw Haw Haw!

...and sinister villains Poison the souls of the meek...

But then...

Haw Haw!

Bomb

a BOMB??? I'LL put my Best men on it!!!

chief

one Tragic Blunder changed their Lives Forever.

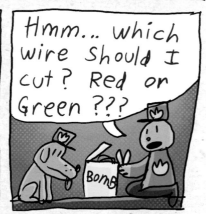

Hmm... which wire should I cut? Red or Green???

Bomb

Grrr!

OK! Green it is!!!

And so.......

SNIP

OH, NO! I Forgot Dogs are Colored Blind!!!

wee-ooo-wee-oo

The doctor had Sad, Sad news.

Boo Hoo.

I'm Sorry, Greg, but your body is dying.

...and Your head is dying too, Cop.

rats!

But just when all seemed lost...

Hey!

← Nurse Lady

Why don't we sew Greg's head onto Cop's Body?

Good idea, nurse Lady! You're a genius!!!

I know.

and soon, a brand new crime fighter was born.

Aw, Man! I unwittingly created the greatest cop of ever!!!!

And it was true. Dog man had the advantages of both man ... and Dog...

...but there was a dark side, too.

Dog Man had some very Bad habits.

He slobbered all over everybody...

chief

Aw, Gross!

...he was obsessed with balls...

squeak squeak squeak

...and for some weird reason, he liked to roll around in dead fish.

aw, man!

not again!

Dog Man, you are a awesome cop.

But you're a **BAD DOGGY!**

You better be a good boy...

...or you'll be in the **DOGHOUSE!**

Will our hero be able to overcome his canine nature and be a better man?

Or will his bad habits get the best of him?

Find Out Now!

If you Like action...

... Suspense...

...Romance...

sniff

sniff

... and Laffs...

chief

Tree House comix Proudly Presents

Chapter 1
The Secret Meeting

by George and Harold

Early one morning at the cop station...

COPS

Dog Man was being very obnoxious.

Hey!

STOP it, DOG Man! LET GO!!!

CUT it OUT!!!

Hey, what's this?

CHIEF's BIRTH-day

and so...

NOW all we need is presents!

What should we get him?

Hmmm... Chief is always forgetting stuff.

I know! Let's get him These "brain Dots" To make him smarTer!!

New SUPA Brain DoTS

Good Thinking!!! What else?

Hmmm...

I know! Chief is very lonely.

Hey! Let's get him a pet to keep him company.

What kind of pet?

How about a ~~dog~~ fish?

Good idea! Fish are awesome pets.

...and they aren't filthy and obnoxious like dogs.

Ok, it's settled!

Dog Man, I'm putting you in charge of buying a fish!

But Remember, Don't buy a dead one!

Chief does **NOT** Like to Roll around in dead fish.

Only **YOU** Like that!

So **Don't** buy a dead one!!!

Hey, we gotta hurry! Chief will be back in **TWO** minutes!

Who wants to go to the pet store?

Who wants to buy a fish?

Who's a good fish buyer???

Dog Man got **SO** excited...

... he **FLIPPED!**

Introducing FLIP-O

BE A FLIP MASTER!

FLIP-O-rama is
Easy if you know the rules:
Flip it, don't rip it!

a haiku
by
Dog Man.

...O-RAMA

EXTRA cheesy

HERE'S HOW iT WORKS:

STEP 1.
First, place your left hand inside the dotted lines marked "Left hand here". Hold the book open FLAT!

STEP 2:
Grasp the right-hand page with your thumb and index finger (inside the dotted lines marked "Right Thumb Here").

STEP 3:
Now quickly flip the right-hand page back and forth until the picture appears to be Animated.

(for extra fun, try adding your own sound-effects!)

Remember,

while you are flipping,
be sure you can see
the images on page 25
AND the images on page 27.

If you flip quickly,
the pictures will
start to look like
one **Animated** cartoon!

Don't forget to
add your own
sound-effects!

Left
hand here.

who wants to go to the pet store?

who wants to buy a fish?

Don't buy a dead one!

Right Thumb here.

Who wants to go to the Pet store?

Who wants to buy a fish?

Don't buy a dead one!

Chapter 2
Penelope's Pets

Penelope's Pets

open

by George and Harold

Ding
Ding

Oh, NO! It's that Dog-headed cop again!

The Pet store People did Not Like Dog Man 'cuz he was a ToTaL pain!!!

DoG BeDs

Boing   Boing!

He sampled all of the Kibbles....

munch munch

DeLuxe BLend

Extra MeaTy

Heav CHUN

...he Licked all of the bones...

DOG Bones on SaLe

30

...and he played with all of the balls.

SQUEAKY BallS

CUT iT OUT, DOG Man!

Look at the mess You made!

IS that any way for a cop to behave?!!?

DOG BoneS On SAle

DELUX

WeLL??? What do you have to say for yourself?!!?

squeak

Gimme That Ball!

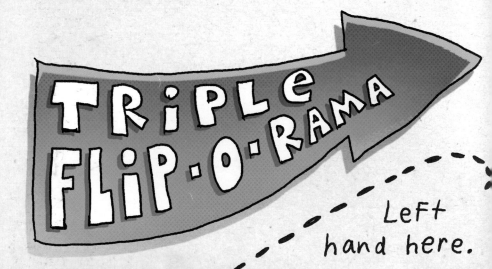

TRiPLe FLiP·O·RAMA

LeFt hand here.

Right
Thumb
here.

OW! My arm!

Then he saw her.

She was beautiful...

...She was fluffy...

... and she smelled great, too.

Sniff
Sniff

Soon, their eyes met.

Can I **HELP** you?

Dog Man Tried
To remember why
he was there.

FiSH
→

Dog Man Looked
at all the Fish.

Then he found
one.

But --- But ---

That fish costs **5** bucks plus tacks!

BuT Dog Man had no money.

A-HA! Just as I suspected!!! Wait Here!

DOG Man wants To buy a fish, but he ain't got no money!!!

Hey, Let's give him that eviL fish.

What eviL fish?

FoLLow me!!!

Empl-oyees onLy

It came to our pet shop last Friday the 13th...

...with a wicked heart and a soul as dark as a thousand midnights!!!!

I tried to put him in with the other fish...

KEEP OUT

...but he took over all of the little castles...

...stole every tiny plastic treasure chest...

DANGER

...and bullied each fish who dared to cross his wretched path!!!

Look upon the fishy face of EVIL!!!

Please Do not tap on glass.

So--- we should give him To Dog Man?

Yeah, why not?

Here you go, DoG Man!

Your very own "Butterfly Fish"!

Hey, it's free— So **NO COMPLAINin'**!

How much is that doggy in the window?

Ding Ding

Oh, that's ZuZu. She's a rescue Dog from The shelter next door.

She's only a hundred bucks PLUS Tacks!

OK! Here's a hundred bucks...

...and here's some Tacks!

awe-some!

THUMB TACKS

Here you go!

CooL!

we're gonna be best friends Forever!!!!!!!

WeLL, Goodbye everyb---

HEY! You're **DOG Man!**

I'm your biggest fan!

CHAPTER 3

HAPPY BIRTHDAY, CHIEF

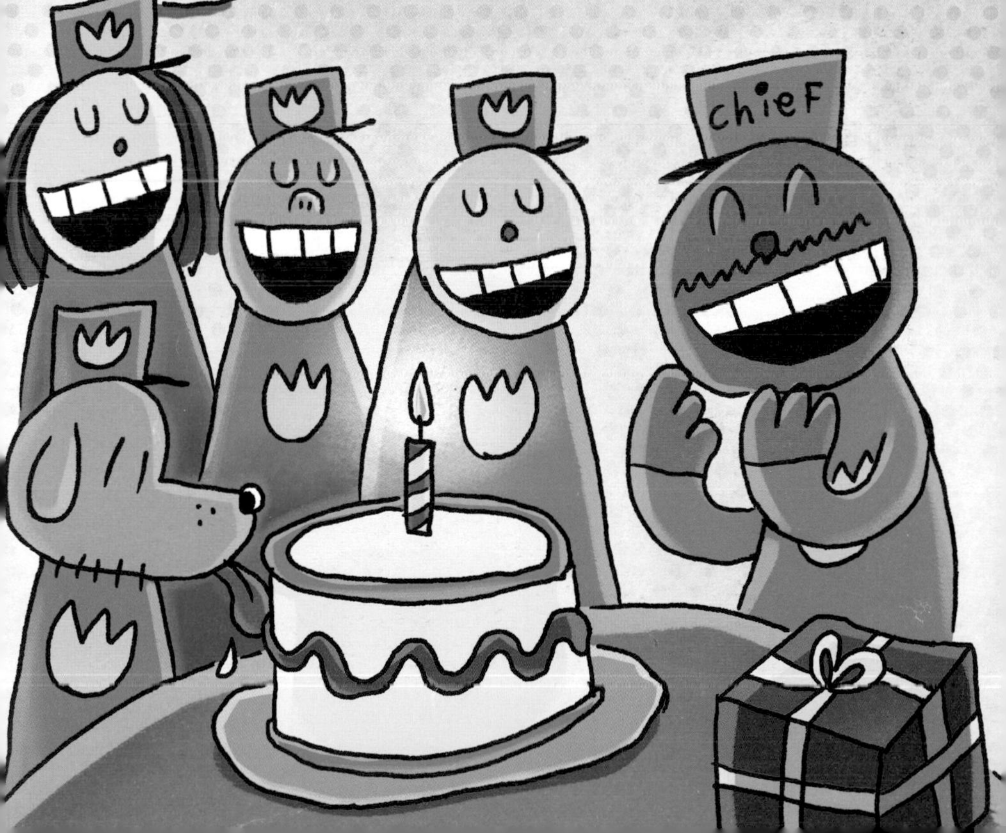

Look What Dog Man got you!

Oh, boy! A fish! I always wanted a fish!!!!

I'm gonna name you FLiPPY!!!

HOORaY!!!

Later....

You can Live here, FLiPPY!

50

one dot

chief

SUpa BWin OTS

chief

I'LL just keep the rest of it up here.

Beep Beep

chief

Hey! It's Time For Lunch!!!

chief

chief's office

-and what happened next?

Well in this book they say:

FLippy's brain grew...

... eleven sizes That day.

ChapTer 4
The BiG
ROBBerY

By George and Harold

One hour Later....

COPS

chief's office

RiNG RiNG

chief's office

RiNG RiNG!

chief

HeLLo?

There's been a Pet store robbery!

where?

at the Pet store!

Oh.

BAD DOGGY!

Dog Man--- The Pet store was <u>Robbed</u>!

Who wants to go to the Pet store?

Does Dog Man wanna go?

Does Dog Man wanna solve the crime???

Who's gonna catch the bad guys?

spin   spin

Lick
Lick
Lick

DOG Bones
on sale

HEY!!!

Oh, Dog Man, it was horrible!!! I came back to buy pet food...

...and a mysterious stranger barged in and tied us up! Then he robbed the store!!!!!

FoRTunately, Zuzu chewed through one of my ropes...

...and I was able to get my ~~hand~~ hand free.

When he wasn't Looking, I Snapped a picture of him on my phone!

What do you think, Dog Man?

...Dog Man ???

Squeaky Balls

Hey!

Hmmm...

Gimme that ball!

Wait a minute...

Chapter 5
Petey's Big Escape

CAT JAIL

One hour Later at cat JaiL...

Pet Shop Robbery
By Sarah Hatoff

Hey, I recognize that guy!

That's **PETEY!!!**

Petey, I'm gonna put you in JaiL!

I already **AM** in Jail !!!!!

But you robbed a store Today!

I haven't even escaped from Jail yet, Today!

Well, too bad! 'Cuz when I catch you....

...I'm gonna put you right back in that cell where you belong!!!

66

I saw this in a book once!

tee-hee!

69

NOOOOOOO!!!

You GoT **FLAT!**

Speak to me!!

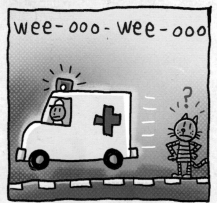

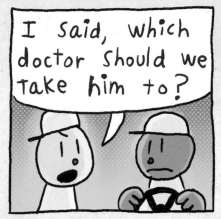

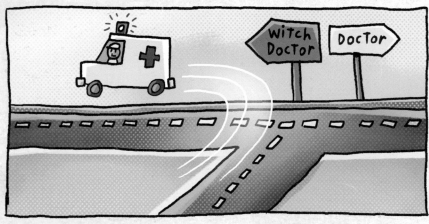

Paper ALWAYS beats Rock!!!

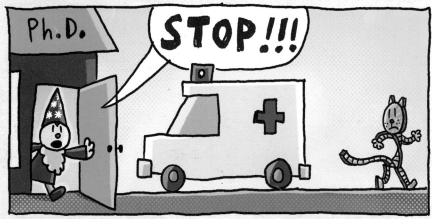

The cloud of spray got closer...

...and Flat Petey had to act fast!

Quickly, he folded his face...

...into the shape of a fan.

FLIP·O·RAMA

Flip like the wind!

Left hand here.

A Fan
with a Plan!

Right
Thumb
here.

A Fan
with a Plan!

Flat Petey's Flipping Fan Face blew the cloud backwards.

chapter 6
A Buncha STUFF That Happened Next

Meanwhile...

Ring Ring

Hi, DOG MaN. It's me, sarah!

I just found ouT a cLue: The Pet store crook didn't steal money!!!

he only stoLe Little Treasure chest**s** !!!

And guess what they were made out of?

Bark!

NO. They were made out of PLASTIC!!!!

I just wrote a story about it on my news blog.

Breaking NEWS
By Sarah Ha

SOON

by Sarah Hatoff
PET STORE CROOK STEALS TREASURE CHESTS... but why?

So--- my impostor is obsessed with Treasure chests, huh?

Hmmm .....

A-HA!!!

I know just how to trap him!

And so...

scrap metal

TRIPLE FLIP-O-RAMA

Left hand here.

Soon, the Treasure Tank 2000 was built.

Now I just need to fill it up with Treasure --- but how?

Of course!!!

invention closet

This "Love Ray" should do the trick!

What's This?

It's a buncha treasure chests filled with gold.

Right. But these aren't **REAL** treasure chests.

huh?

This is just a buncha plastic toys, right?

They're not real gold, right?

They're **NOT**???

Real treasure chests are wooden and filled with gold, right? Like that one on TV.

Haw! Haw! Haw!

C'mon everybody! Fill this chest up with your treasure and stuff!!!

Oh, NO!!! Petey the cat is forcing people to fill his treasure chest with loot!

No I'm not!!!

Tree House Comix Proudly Presents

Chapter 7

BiG FiGHT

By George and Harold

Soon things began to get out of control.

Petey was zapping everybody with his Love ray.

ZAP!

...and everybody was falling under his spell.

ZAP!

We Love ya, Petey!!!

Dog Man stood atop a nearby building, watching the Tragedy unfold beneath him.

Haw Haw!

Quickly, he reached in his shirt...

... and pulled out his fav-orite bone.

Lick Lick Lick...

Dog Man tied a string to his bone...

... and gave it a toss.

whoosh!

whoosh!

Clank!

Dog Man gave the string a tug...

... and then ...

suddenLy...

HEY! How'd Y<u>ou</u> get over there?

You Let go of that Controller **RIGHT NOW!**

That is **<u>NOT</u>** a ball!

That's a Sophisticated...

Yank!

P-Piece of ---

machinery!

TRIPLE FLIP·O· RAMA

Left hand here.

Right
Thumb
here.

Uh-oh!

KLUNK!

Petey! are you OK???

ChapTer 8
FLAT CAT FeveR

Meanwhile, back in town, Tensions were still high...

Dog Man would not let go of the ball.

Sarah Tried to convince him...

Drop the Ball, DOG Man!!!!

Zuzu Tried, too!

RuFF! RuFF! RuFF!

Even Chief couldn't make Dog Man Listen to reason.

BAD DOGGY

Gimme that can of "Living Spray"!

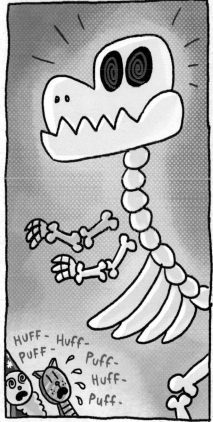

HUFF-
PUFF-
HUFF-
PUFF-
HUFF-
PUFF.

ALRight, Listen up, bub! From now on, you have to obey ME!!!

And I order you To **DESTROY DOG MAN!!!**

FLIP·O·RAMA

Cheesy Animation Technology...

Left hand here.

JurassiC Bark

Right
Thumb
here.

Jurassic Bark

It Looked Like this was the end for DOG Man...

Everyone was terrified...

...but then...

Zuzu got a idea.

133

DOG MAN---

It's BONES!

IT's BONES!

SKELETONS are Made OUT OF BONES!!!

when Dog man Realized the truth...

...He stopped being afraid.

screech

Dog man **LOVED** bones!!!

so he just did what came naturally.

Lick

Lick Lick Lick

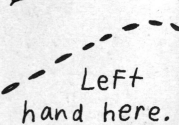

Left hand here.

Chapter 9
The MYSTERIOUS STRANGER RETURNS

Who I am is not important...

... the important thing is what I can **DO**!

The mysterious stranger used his mind powers to pick up a phone booth.

Phone Phone

what's a Phone booth?

Beats me!

The mysterious stranger then levitated a stack of newspapers.

What's a newspaper?

Beats me.

BONK!

Next, he grabbed a mailbox.

What's a mailbox?

Beats me!

KLAK

Then he grabbed some other stuff with his brain.

Things were
beginning to
seem hopeless...

...Until Zuzu came
up with a plan!

ZUZU--- NOOO!!!!

Earlier Today,
I was minding my
own business....

...When I heard
a loud Sound...

...Followed by a lot
of little Sounds.

PLip PLip PLip PLip
PLip PLip PLip
PLip PLip PLip
PLip PLip
PLip PLip PLip PLip
PLip PLip PLip

Suddenly, my brain
began to think
like never before.

I became aware
of universes beyond
my own...

Soon, I found that
I could move things
with my **MiNd.**

Soon, they reached the top of the mountain.

Hey, you guys missed all the fun!

Poor widdle Flippy!

He was so excited, he forgot all about how water freezes up here!

I--- I've --- got ---to g--- get ---

With his last bit of Supa Brain Power...

... Flippy raised the book and speed-read every page.

I've --- j-j-just --- discovered --- how I --- c-c-c-can Live --- f-forever!!!

ALL --- I --- N-Need T-T-To --- d-d-do --- is c-c-c-concentrate!

Flippy calmed his mind and focused...

... deeper and deeper he concentrated...

Soon, FLiPPy's SouL was transformed into pure energy.

IT Worked!!!

But I must act QuicKLy!!!

According to that book, I've only got TWO minutes to Transfer my SouL inTo somebody else!

Then I can snatch their body and Live forever!!!

I Think I'LL Snatch Chief's Body!!!

Run, chief, Run!

Go ahead and try!!!

You can't outrun a ball of pure energy!!!

When Dog Man heard the word "baLL"....

... he stopped being afraid...

... and just did what came naturally!

166

You destroyed my Car !!!

Now how are we supposed to get offa this Mountain?

You're **NOT!**

You're supposed to **FREEZE!**

Let's face it---
I WON!!!

What could **YOU** POSSIBLY have To say ?!!?

WeLL? Spit it Out, Man!!!!

AW, GROSS! You got Dog slobber all over me!!!

Now I'm all wet---

---And C-C-Cold!!!

Flat Petey was RIGHT --- Paper DOESN'T freeze...

...but **WET** Paper freezes very QuickLy!!!

FOOMP

Flat Petey was now a thick sheet of ice.

Dog Man climbed aboard.

And soon...

175

The whole gang zipped to the bottom of the mountain...

...Laughing all the way.

HA-HA-HA-HA-HAW-HAW HA-HA HA

Hey! My 'Obey Spray' wore off!

Ain't you glad you ain't gotta obey nobody no more?

I sure amn't!

But there was one person who wasn't glad at all...

HEY!!!

You guys froze me and used me Like a snowboard!

Now I'm all scratched up!!!

You can't treat Paper Like that!!!

Flat Petey, have you ever played Rock, Paper, Scissors?

I'm **AWARE** of the game — Why?

TRiPLE SNiP-O-RAMA

Left hand here.

Shear
Terror

Don't get
SNippy
with Me!

I Like
Big cuts
and I
cannot
Lie.

Right
Thumb
here.

Shear
Terror

Don't get
SNippy
with Me!

I Like
Big cuts
and I
cannot
Lie.

Good boy, DOG man!

You're our hero!

HOORAY FOR DOG MAN!

EPILOGUE

The BEST BiRTHdAY EVER!

BUT WAIT...

...if you thought our adventure was over...

YOU Ain't READ **NOThin' YeT!**

AT this very moment, George and Harold are busy making their **NEXT** Dog Man Epic noveL...

check it out!!!

DOG MAN
A TALE OF TWO KITTIES

He was the best of Dogs...

...he was the worst of Dogs.

It was the age of invention...

...it was the season of surprise.

It was the eve of Supa Sadness.

it was the dawn of hope.

free kitty

What the Dickens is Going on ?!!?

If you Like action...

... and Thrills...

... and Laffs...

BONUS COMIX ➤

This next comic was something we made bAck when we were in Kindergarten!

... back in the carefree days of our youths.

Ahhh, I remember them well.

Juice boxes... nap time...

... safety scissors... scented markers...

sniff

MEMORIES!!!

Tree House Comix Inc. presents

DOG Man

and The wrath of Petey

Action

Drama

Laffs

a epic novella by
George Beard and
Harold Hutchins

DOG man was awesome but He sure was stinky!!!

P.U.

YoU Need a Bath, DOG Man!

OWOOOWOOOWOOWOOO

?

How come He ran a way?

Don't YoU Know? aLL DOGS Hate BathS!!!!

OH yeah I FORGOT.

Petey went on a crime spree

Haw Haw

He robbed Banks.

aw, man!

$

Jim's Bank

Jim

He stole Jewels

Gimme!

no fair

He even Hi-Jacked cars

STOP, thief!

Yee Haa!

But no cops could ever catch him

Haw Haw

Gee, I sure wish Dog man would come Back!

me too.

meanwhile, DOG Man was Hiding in a alley

munch munch

Trash can

Then...

NEWS

PETEY Runs amuck

BUT where is DOG man huh?

Trash can

DOG man Felt ashamed.

He Knew he Must Be Brave

So DOG man Returned Bravishly To save the Day

Dog Man searched for Petey

Soon He picked up a trail.

snif snif

It Led Straight to Petey's Hideout.

snif snif snif

Petey the world's most evilest cat

But it was a trap

guess what?

It's Bath Time

spray

DOG man DUG all the way under the zoo.

He came up in the skunk cage.

PETEY RAN OUT OF THE HOLE

RIGHT INTO A COP'S NET

got-cha

YOU'RE GOING TO JAIL, BUSTER

rats!

FLIP-O-rama
Here's ☒ How 2 do it.

PUT YOUR Left Hand There on Dotted Line

HOLD THE other page with your thumb

Flip the page Back and Forth

It makes it look Like a moving cartoon

Left Hand Here

Bathtime
For
Dog man

RIGHT
THUMB
HERE

Bathtime
For
Dog man

So Petey went back to cat jail,

rats!

and Dog Man learned his lesson.

You smell great!

SNIFF SNIFF

Hooray for Dog Man!

Hey!

THE END

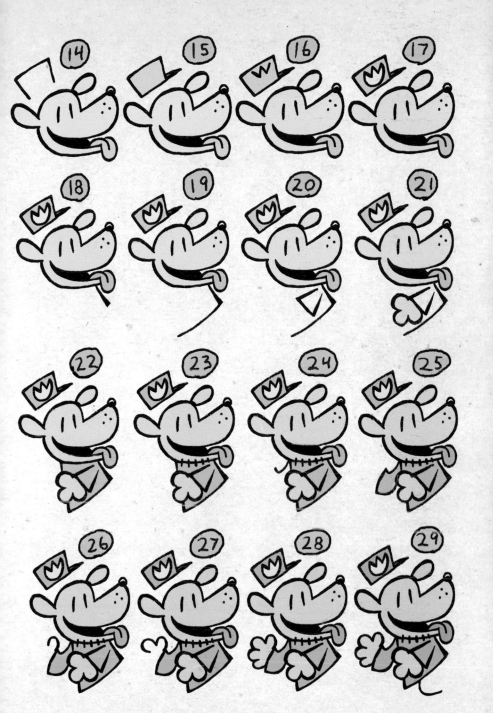

HOW 2 DRAW FLAT PETEY

...in 8 more Ridiculously easy steps!

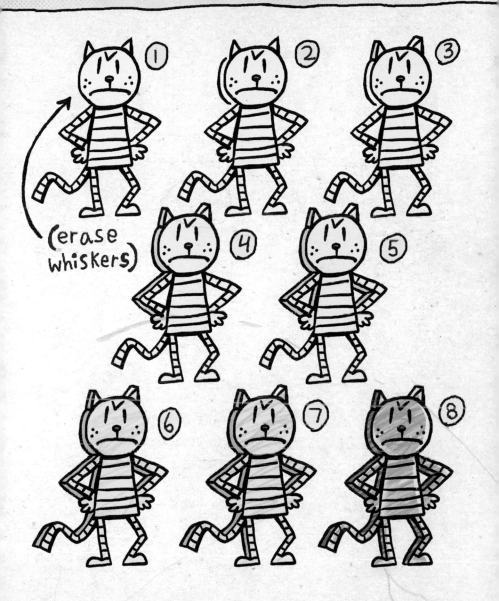

(erase whiskers)

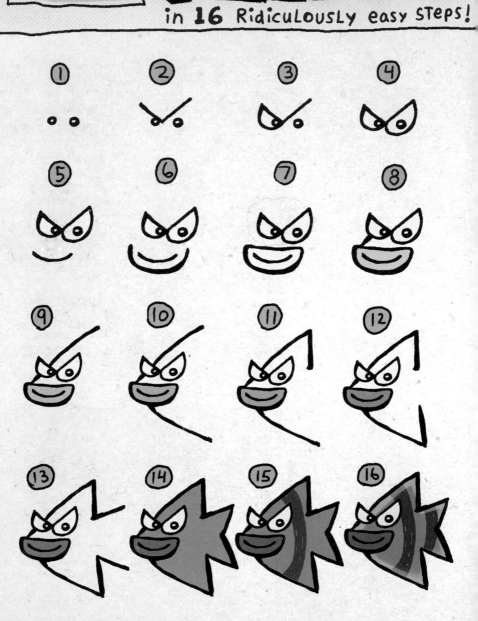

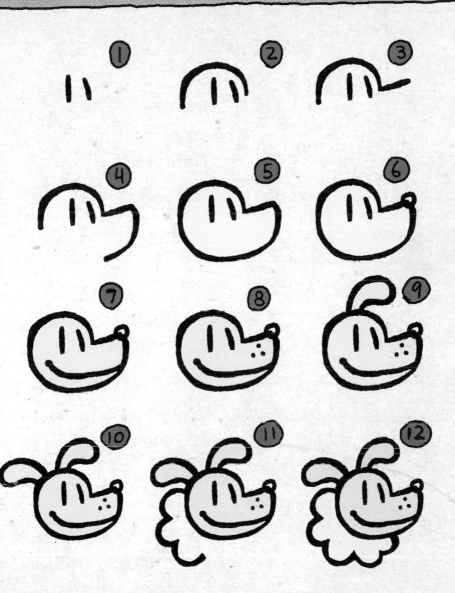

BUT WAIT!

the Fun continues online!!!

GAMES

Make your own FLIP-O-RAMAS!

CRAFTS

Learn to draw SARAH, Chief, and MORE!

Videos

at **PiLKEY.COM** and **ScholaStic.com/PLANETPiLKEY**

ABOUT THE AUTHOR-ILLUSTRATOR

When Dav Pilkey was a kid, he suffered from ADHD, dyslexia, and behavioral problems. Dav was so disruptive in class that his teachers made him sit out in the hall every day. Luckily, Dav loved to draw and make up stories. He spent his time in the hallway creating his own original comic books.

In the second grade, Dav Pilkey created a comic book about a superhero named Captain Underpants. His teacher ripped it up and told him he couldn't spend the rest of his life making silly books.

Fortunately, Dav was not a very good listener.

ABOUT THE COLORIST

Jose Garibaldi grew up on the South Side of Chicago. As a kid, he was a daydreamer and a doodler, and now it's his full-time job to do both. Jose is a professional illustrator, painter, and cartoonist who has created work for Dark Horse Comics, Disney, Nickelodeon, MAD Magazine, and many more. He lives in Los Angeles, California, with his wife and their cats.